AMELIA BEDELIA
AND THE BABY

by PEGGY PARISH

Pictures by Lynn Sweat

AN AVON  CAMELOT BOOK

3rd Grade reading level has been determined by using the Fry Readability Scale.

AVON BOOKS
A division of
The Hearst Corporation
1350 Avenue of the Americas
New York, New York 10019

Text copyright © 1981 by Margaret Parish
Illustrations copyright © 1981 by Lynn Sweat
Published by arrangement with Greenwillow Books, a division of William Morrow and Company, Inc.
Library of Congress Catalog Card Number: 80-22263
ISBN: 0-380-72795-1

First Avon Camelot Reformat Printing: July 1996
First Avon Camelot Printing: May 1982

CAMELOT TRADEMARK REG. U.S. PAT. OFF. AND IN OTHER COUNTRIES, MARCA REGISTRADA, HECHO EN U.S.A.

Printed in the U.S.A.

QH 10 9 8 7 6 5 4 3 2

Avon Books are available at special quantity discounts for bulk purchases for sales promotions, premiums, fund raising or educational use. Special books, or book excerpts, can also be created to fit specific needs.

For details write or telephone the office of the Director of Special Markets, Avon Books, Dept. FP, 1350 Avenue of the Americas, New York, New York 10019, 1-800-238-0658.

For Jennifer and Jay Thompson,

with love

—P.P.

For Peggy

—L.S.

"But Mrs. Rogers,"
said Amelia Bedelia.
"I don't know a thing
about babies.
How can I babysit?"
"Why, Amelia Bedelia!"
said Mrs. Rogers.
"You are very good
with children."
"Yes," said Amelia Bedelia.
"I get along fine
with children."

"Babies are children, too,"
said Mrs. Rogers.
"If you say so,"
said Amelia Bedelia.
"Now you run along,"
said Mrs. Rogers.
"Mrs. Lane is waiting."

So Amelia Bedelia ran
to Mrs. Lane's house.

She knocked on the door.

"Do come in," said Mrs. Lane.

"I'm already late.

Here is your list.
I hope I didn't forget anything.
But you will know what to do."
"I will?" said Amelia Bedelia.

"I gave Missy her lunch,"
said Mrs. Lane.
"She is in her playpen."
Mrs. Lane left.
"How about that?"
said Amelia Bedelia.
"Babies are kept in pens."
Amelia Bedelia found Missy.
"Hi, Missy," she said.

Missy looked at Amelia Bedelia.
She began to cry.
"Oh, oh," said Amelia Bedelia.
"What should I do?
What does the list say?"

Amelia Bedelia read,
"Give Missy a bottle."

She hurried to the kitchen.
Then she stopped.
"That can't be right,"
said Amelia Bedelia.
"Babies shouldn't have bottles.
They could break."

She thought a bit.
"I know," she said.
"I'll give her a can
or maybe a box."

Missy howled louder.
"I'll give her both,"
said Amelia Bedelia.
And she did.

Missy picked up the can.
She threw it.
She picked up the box.
She threw it.
And she howled.

"All right," said Amelia Bedelia.
"I'll find something else."
She gave Missy one thing
after another.
But Missy just howled louder.

"Maybe you are hungry,"
said Amelia Bedelia.
"I'll get you a cookie."
She ran to the kitchen.
The back door opened.
"Anybody home?"
called Mrs. Carter.

"I'm here," said Amelia Bedelia.
"Here are some strawberries,"
said Mrs. Carter.
"I hear Missy.
Why is she crying?"
"Beats me," said Amelia Bedelia.
"I'm at my wit's end."
"Have you given her a bottle?"
said Mrs. Carter.
"A bottle!" said Amelia Bedelia.
"I have not."

"I think that is what
she wants," said Mrs. Carter.
"I will fix one for her.
You put the strawberries
in something else.
I need my basket."
"All right," said Amelia Bedelia.

Soon Mrs. Carter said,
"The bottle is ready."
"Good," said Amelia Bedelia.
"Here is your basket."
Mrs. Carter left.

Amelia Bedelia looked at the bottle.
"Always something new," she said.
"This bottle won't break.
It's just fine for babies."

She gave the bottle
to Missy.
Missy stopped crying.
"I am glad to know about
those bottles," said Amelia Bedelia.
"They do shush up babies."

Missy finished her bottle.
Amelia Bedelia looked at the list.
"Good," she said.
"You get a bath now.
I know about that."
Amelia Bedelia got
everything ready.
She put Missy in the tub.

Soon Missy was all clean.
"That's done," said Amelia Bedelia.
"Back into your pen you go."
Amelia Bedelia got the list.
She read, "Be sure
to use the baby powder."
She found the powder.

And Amelia Bedelia used it.

"My, I smell good," she said.
"That was nice of Mrs. Lane.
Now what does she want me to do?"
She looked at the list.

"From two until three
is naptime," said Amelia Bedelia.
She shook her head.
"No!" said Amelia Bedelia.
"I won't do it.
I won't take a nap. I hate naps!"

Amelia Bedelia thought a bit.
Then she said, "I know!
Those strawberries!
I will make a surprise.
I do make good strawberry tarts."

She started for the kitchen.
"First," she said,
"I'll see what Missy is doing."
She went to the playpen.

"How about that!
Missy likes naps,"
said Amelia Bedelia.
"She can take mine for me.
I've got better things to do."

She went to the kitchen.
She put some of this
and a little of that
into a bowl.

She mixed and mixed.
Soon her tarts were made.
"Those do look pretty,"
she said.

She put the tarts away.
Missy began to cry.
"Missy is awake,"
said Amelia Bedelia.
"Let me see what
I should do."

"It says to give her
a mashed banana," she said.
"That will be easy."
She got a banana.
And she mashed it.
"This is fun," said Amelia Bedelia.
"But I better give it to Missy."

Missy took the banana.
She looked at it.
Then she mashed it.

She mashed it harder and harder.
Suddenly the skin popped.
Banana squished all over Missy.

Missy clapped her hands.
Then she ate the squishy banana.
Amelia Bedelia laughed.
"I never saw anything like
that before," she said.
"But she had fun.
And it was her banana."

Then Missy began to fuss.
"I can forget the list for now,"
said Amelia Bedelia.
"I know what you need.
You need another bath."

So Missy got another bath.
"Babies do need a lot of washing,"
said Amelia Bedelia.
She dressed Missy.
"Now back to the list," she said.

"Put Missy
in her stroller,"
she read.
Amelia Bedelia
did that.
Then she read,
"But first, put a sweater on her."

Amelia Bedelia
took Missy
out of the stroller.
"Your mama should
have said that first,"
said Amelia Bedelia.

She put a sweater on Missy.
"Back in you go," she said.

She looked at the list again.
"Tarnation!" she said.
"Your mama can't make
up her mind. Now she says
to take you out for a while."

Amelia Bedelia took Missy
out of the stroller.
"In and out. In and out,"
she said. "I'm plumb tired."

Amelia Bedelia put Missy
in her playpen.
She looked at the list.
"You must be out for good,"
she said.

"It says playtime is
until five o'clock.
Now that is a treat.
I don't get to play much."
Amelia Bedelia looked
around.
"Now what shall I play?"
she said.
She saw Missy's toy box.
"Look at all the toys!"
she said.

Amelia Bedelia sat down.
She began to play.
She played first with one toy.
Then she played with another.
"Oh, what fun!" she said.
"I wish I had toys like these."

Missy began to fuss.
Amelia Bedelia looked
at her watch.
"Shoot!" she said.
"It's five o'clock.
Playtime is over."
She put away the toys.

Then she looked at the list.
"It's time for your supper,"
she said.
"The list says I should
give you some baby food."
Amelia Bedelia picked up Missy.
They went to the kitchen.
Amelia Bedelia put Missy
in her chair.

She took off Missy's sweater
and then read from the list,
"Don't forget
to put on Missy's bib."
Amelia Bedelia found the bib.
"That's plumb cute," she said.
And Amelia Bedelia put it on.

"Now," she said,
"I'll make your supper."
Amelia Bedelia scurried around.
She made baby hamburgers.

She cooked baby potatoes.

She sliced baby tomatoes.

"That is a good supper,"
said Amelia Bedelia.
She started to give it to Missy.
"Oh, oh," she said. "The catsup.
I forgot the catsup."
She poured catsup
over everything.
"Children do love catsup,"
said Amelia Bedelia.
She gave Missy her supper.
Missy tasted it. She smiled.
And Missy ate her supper.

Amelia Bedelia laughed.

"You really liked that," she said.

"You will like this, too."

Amelia Bedelia got a strawberry tart.

"Here," she said.

Missy grabbed the tart.
She ate all of that, too.
"You are a mess,"
said Amelia Bedelia.
"You need washing again."

Mr. and Mrs. Lane came in.
"My baby!" said Mrs. Lane.
"What did you do to her?
What is that red stuff?"
"Red stuff?" said Amelia Bedelia.

"Oh, some of it is catsup,"
she said.
"The rest is strawberries."
"Catsup! Strawberries!"
said Mrs. Lane.
"She can't eat things like that."

"Oh, yes she can,"
said Amelia Bedelia.
"She loves them."
"Why did I leave Missy with you!"
said Mrs. Lane.
"You don't know a thing
about babies."

Mr. Lane ate a strawberry tart.
"Delicious," he said.
"Don't you ever—"
said Mrs. Lane.

But that was as far as she got.
Her mouth was full
of strawberry tart.
"My favorite!" she said.

Missy began to cry.

Mrs. Lane went to her.

But Missy wanted Amelia Bedelia.

"She never did that before,"
said Mr. Lane.

"Amelia Bedelia must know
something we don't."

"I think she knows a lot,"
said Mrs. Lane.

"I'm sorry I got angry.
Will you come again?"

"I would love to,"
said Amelia Bedelia.
"But I have to go now."

Amelia Bedelia walked home.
"I declare," she said.
"That was plumb fun.
Babies are real people.
And I get along
just fine with them."